Zin! Zin! Zin! a Violin

By Lloyd Moss

Illustrated by Marjorie Priceman

SIMON & SCHUSTER BOOKS FOR YOUNG READERS
An imprint of Simon & Schuster Children's Publishing Division
1230 Avenue of the Americas, New York, New York 10020
Text copyright © 1995 by Lloyd Moss.
Illustrations copyright © 1995 by Marjorie Priceman.
Reprinted by arrangement with Simon & Schuster Books for Young
Readers, Simon & Schuster's Children's Publishing Division
SIMON & SCHUSTER BOOKS FOR YOUNG READERS
is a trademark of Simon & Schuster. Designed by Paul Zakris.
The text for this book is set in 15 ½-point Joanna Bold.
The illustrations were done in gouache.
Printed in China
10 9 8 7 6

Library of Congress Cataloging-in-Publication Data
Moss, Lloyd.
    Zin! zin! zin! : a violin / by Lloyd Moss ; illustrated by Marjorie Priceman
        p.   cm.
    Summary: Ten instruments take their parts one by one in a
musical performance.
    [1. Musical instruments—Fiction.   2. Music—Fiction.   3. Counting.
4. Stories in rhyme.]   I. Priceman, Marjorie, ill.   II. Title.
PZ8.3.M8464Zi   1995   [E]—dc20   93-37902   CIP   AC
ISBN: 0-671-88239-2

To Anne, Bradley, Brice, Liana, Nanette—
the music and the poetry in my life
—L. M.

For Jonah Squirsky and his descendants
—M. P.

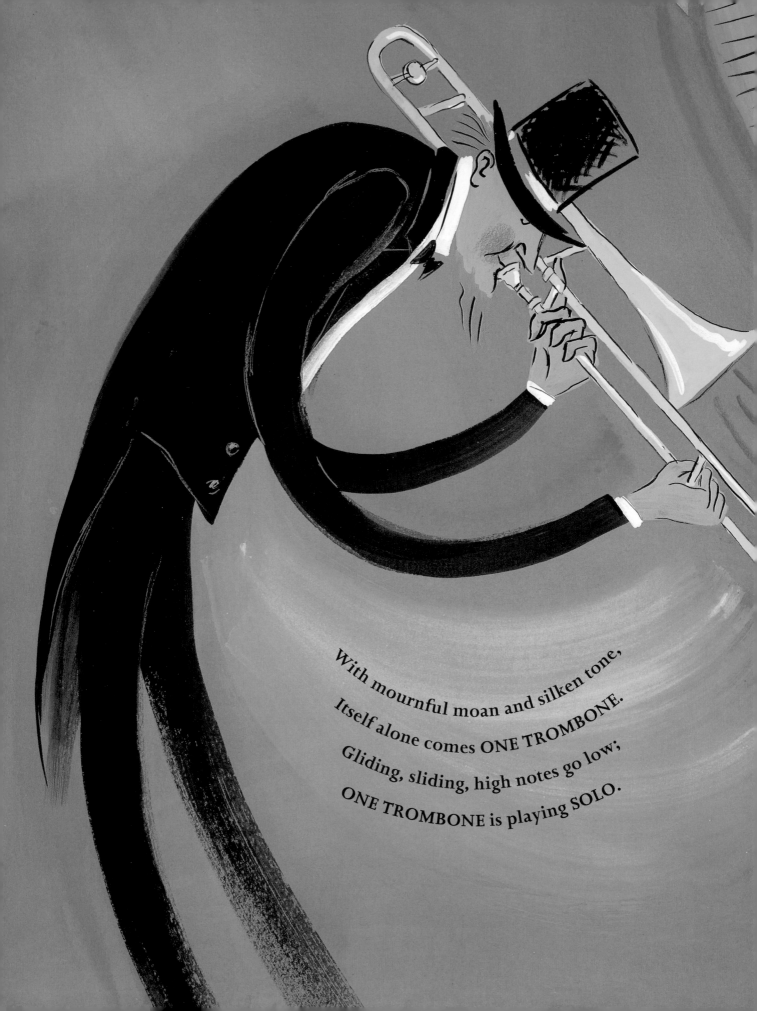

With mournful moan and silken tone,
Itself alone comes ONE TROMBONE.
Gliding, sliding, high notes go low;
ONE TROMBONE is playing SOLO.

Next, a TRUMPET comes along,

And sings and stings its swinging song.

It joins TROMBONE, no more alone,

And ONE and TWO-O, they're a DUO.

Fine FRENCH HORN, its valves all oiled,
Bright and brassy, loops all coiled,
Golden yellow; joins its fellows.
TWO, now THREE-O, what a TRIO!

Now, a mellow friend, the CELLO,
Neck extended, bows a "hello";
End pin set upon the floor,
It makes up a QUARTET—that's FOUR.

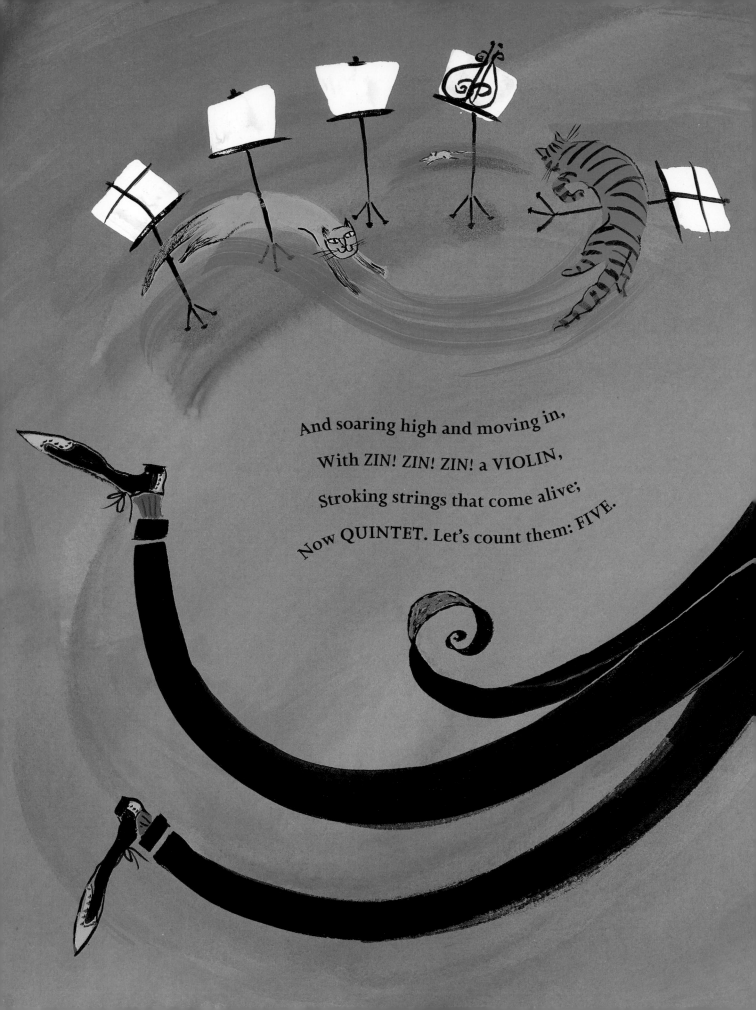

And soaring high and moving in,

With ZIN! ZIN! ZIN! a VIOLIN,

Stroking strings that come alive;

Now QUINTET. Let's count them: FIVE.

FLUTE, that sends our soul a-shiver;

FLUTE, that slender, silver sliver.

A place among the set it picks

To make a young SEXTET—that's SIX.

With steely keys that softly click,
Its breezy notes so darkly slick,
A sleek, black, woody CLARINET
Is number SEVEN—now SEPTET.

Gleeful, bleating, sobbing, pleading,

Through its throbbing double-reeding;

OBOE, please don't hesitate:

Come, make it an OCTET—that's EIGHT.

That lazy clown, the big BASSOON!
He plays low down, we're laughing soon.
Here, Grumpy, get your place in line,
And give us a NONET—that's NINE.

The HARP descends with angel's wings,

A heaven's blend through magic strings,

And when it joins the others, then

Behold! A CHAMBER GROUP of TEN.

The ORCHESTRA comes in the hall.
They're on the stage; we see them all:
The CELLO, HARP, and CLARINET,
The TRUMPET, whom we've also met,
The OBOE, FLUTE, and big BASSOON,
All eager to get started soon.
TROMBONE, FRENCH HORN, and VIOLIN,
All poised and ready. Now, begin!

The STRINGS all soar, the REEDS implore,
The BRASSES roar with notes galore.
It's music that we all adore.
It's what we go to concerts for.

The minutes fly, the music ends,
And so, good-bye to our new friends.
But when they've bowed and left the floor,
If we clap loud and shout, "Encore!"
They may come out and play once more.

And that would give us great delight
Before we say a late good night.